Samuel French Acting Edition

Frontieres Sans Frontieres

by Phillip Howze

SAMUELFRENCH.COM   SAMUELFRENCH.CO.UK

MUSIC USE NOTE

Licensees are solely responsible for obtaining formal written permission from copyright owners to use copyrighted music in the performance of this play and are strongly cautioned to do so. If no such permission is obtained by the licensee, then the licensee must use only original music that the licensee owns and controls. Licensees are solely responsible and liable for all music clearances and shall indemnify the copyright owners of the play(s) and their licensing agent, Samuel French, against any costs, expenses, losses and liabilities arising from the use of music by licensees. Please contact the appropriate music licensing authority in your territory for the rights to any incidental music.

All instances of incidental music are optional. The two instances of sung music ("Fitted Panties" on pp. 21 and 48) are required for performance. Music for these two songs is included in the back of this acting edition.

Author's Note on Incidental Music

Any instances of music throughout this play are guideposts.

Be encouraged to enact your wild imagination. Be mindful, but also inspired and playful.

In the original production, the Choir was a half-dozen teenagers, all young people of color.

IMPORTANT BILLING AND CREDIT REQUIREMENTS

If you have obtained performance rights to this title, please refer to your licensing agreement for important billing and credit requirements.

FRONTIERES SANS FRONTIERES was first produced by The Bushwick Starr (Noel Allain, Artistic Director; Sue Kessler, Executive Director) in Brooklyn, New York from March 1-25, 2017. The production was directed by Dustin Wills, with sets by Mariana Sanchez Hernandez, costumes by Seth Bodie, sound design by Nok Chanabanca, lighting design by Masha Tsimring, flight by Grounded Aerial, and technical direction by Jen Medina Gray. The co-producers were Libby Peterson, Sally Shen, and Alyssa Simmons. The production stage manager was Alyssa K. Howard. The cast was as follows:

WIN	Emma Ramos
NOON / NOBLE LAUREATE	Mirirai Sithole
PAN	Tony Vo
THOM	Sathya Sridharan
BACKPACKER / BABY BOO / MIME	Mitchell Winter
CIGARETTE MAN / DEVELOPER	Reggie D. White
W.H.O. / CLOWN	Ceci Fernandez
ACTRESS / MILITIA	Rachel Leslie
CHOIR	Ayesha Benjamin, Dana Colyer, Sophia M. T. Davis, Azure Hurley, Nicky Ooyama, Aiden Raheb, Novahliz Rose

CHARACTERS

WIN – a young girl who dresses as a boy, a mimic, a trickster
NOON – a young girl who dresses as a girl (later, Noble Laureate)
PAN – a young boy who dresses in whatever clothes he can find
THOM – a foreigner who dresses like a foreigner

as well as

BACKPACKER – a foreigner who dresses like a local
CIGARETTE MAN – a foreigner with cancer
W.H.O. – a bureaucrat
BABY BOO – a pop star
ACTRESS – an ambassador
MILITIA – a soldier
DEVELOPER – a planner
NOBLE LAUREATE – a winner
CLOWN – a clown
MIME – a mime

SETTING

Here.
Where is Here?
Here is Here.

At the center outskirts, immediately to the eastwest of the South-South.

Everyone who lives Here speaks in all sorts of dialects and accents.

A few of the accents are familiar-specific,
though some seem vague-familiar.
Several, however, may be brand-new-unfamiliar or yet to be invented.

Every accent, no matter how extraordinary, should always favor the studied articulation of Engaleash.

ON STAGING

The world should feel like the intersection of ours and theirs; familiar and foreign.

The heart of this play is located in the art of commedia and physicality.

Work with integrity, humor, delight, spectacle, boundless compassion, zero earnestness.

Cast only people of color in these roles.

This // indicates where a line overlaps with the following line.

ACKNOWLEDGEMENTS

Thank you to Sarah Ruhl, Paula Vogel, Jeanie O'Hare, Ken Prestininzi, Anne Erbe, Zack Klim, Maureen Aung-Thwin, Mike Paller, Jeffrey Stein, Zaw Zaw, Heather Marciniec, Liz Tydeman, Maria-Cristina Aragon, William Burke, Mallery Avidon, Knud Adams, Jay Owen Eisenberg, Prema Cruz, Mariko Nakosone, Megan Hill, Jennifer Tsay, Gabe Levey, Ugo Chukwu, Ephraim Birney, April Matthis, Zenzi Williams, David Shih, Ngozi Anyanwu, Alex Tobey, Nick Auer, Scotty Anderson, Eliza Simpson, Kevin Klakouski, John King, Ien Denio, Ian Douglas-Moore, the awesome parents of our youth choir members.

Landfill. Dump site
Garbage garbages everywhere
So grotesque like glitters
Waste landed treasure chest
Heaps to memorial lost forgotten lives

Bugle!
Bright bugle!
Bugle becomes tuba
Sad sad tuba

Children of Dump rush in: **WIN** *and* **NOON** *and* **PAN**
They eyes glitters brights besides garbages
Appear them too be tiny revolting looking angels

Farts!

Pause
Joy music! The children to dance!
Disco light

Pause
Bomb in far off. Breathe
Go

Happy music!
The children to dance!

Pause
Cry babies. Gunfire. Bloodlet. Murmur a revolution
Go

Music music!
The children to dance
Disco light

Black
Bomb
Heavy breath breathe
Heavy breath breathing

Light

NOON *and* **PAN** *run run round. Quick and verying*

Run running and to fall on knees arms outreach wide

Stopping catching breathing

WIN *to pace hold tiny twig*

WIN.

Agin.

> *Same same run a game it*
>
> **NOON** *and* **PAN** *runn running falling knees*
>
> *They out reach deep, longer necks touch to sky try*

WIN.

Okay okay fine finnish.

> **PAN** *and* **NOON** *stop for breatheless*

WIN.

Nice is Noon.

Pan?

–

Now. Watch.

Numbah. One.

> **WIN** *is pose No. 01: frail & diminutive & determined*

WIN.

Okay?

Numbah. Two.

> **WIN** *is posing No. 02: concave stomach & crip walk & poignant*

WIN.

You see?

Now.

–

Numba. Three.

> **WIN** *are pose No. 03: bright eyes & asthmatic & messianic*
>
> **WIN** *to stopping posing breatheless*
>
> **NOON** *and* **PAN** *claps*

WIN.

Yeahyeah.

Okay, ready you.

Ready?

Numbah one.

> **NOON** *and* **PAN** *pose No. 01*

WIN.

HmmOkay gooood.

Noobah two!

> **NOON** *and* **PAN** *pose No. 02*

WIN.

(Adjust to **PAN***)* Mmhmm.

And, Numbar three.

> **NOON** *and* **PAN** *pose No. 03*

WIN.

Pan, you more sadly to please.

–

More sadly?

–

More?

> **WIN** *pull to* **PAN** *ear*

PAN.

Ow!

WIN.

Ooo "ow"? Bettah.

Okay too fast?

NOON & PAN.

Okay! // yeas yeas.

WIN.

–

Numba one!

> **NOON-PAN** *pose*

WIN.

Noombar three!

Namba one!

Noombah two.

Nobar one.

Nobar one!

Nobar… one!

Numba two!

Numba four!

> *(Stop. Fast laugh. Go!)*

Numba two! One! Three! Two! Three! One! Two!One twothree! Onetwothreethree!
One twothree oneone threeone onetwo onethreetwotwothreethreetwotwothree!
Ah, seeee! You must to be fast. Like shadow. Like never-ever was there.
Undastand?

NOON & PAN.

Yeas okay, mmhm // Fine.

WIN.

Yeas…what?

NOON & PAN.

Yesa, sir!

WIN.

Mhm.

Fin fini. Nownow, Engaleash pratict.

Say: "Apple."

NOON.

Apple.

PAN.

Apple.

WIN.

A apples.

NOON & PAN.

A apples.

WIN.

A applez is two applez will be's manys applez trees.

NOON.

A apples is two applez
will be's manys applez // trees.

PAN.

A apples is two…
Mangoes.

WIN.

(To **PAN***)* Eh, applesuh.

And?

"You do have apple one? I do like apple."

NOON.

You do have apple one?
I do –

PAN.

(Joy, crip walk) You do have I do
like it mango.

WIN.

Pan you mouth to say I do like apple.

PAN.

But do not like a apple my mouth is like uh mango.

WIN.

O. You know Engaleash?

PAN.

Yeas.

No.

– *(Smile)*

Little.

WIN.

Yes no little?

Me I know big.

I, Win, hm?

PAN.

–

Yeas.

WIN.

I know speaking Engaleash?

PAN.

Mhm.

WIN.

You want learning Engaleash impress to foreigner?

PAN.

I-like-mango.

WIN.

Eh-eh, say "apple" okay?

Apple are rare.

Mango? Everywhere in here.

Apple: expense. Mango be free.

Apple, mm mm. Mango, meh-meh.

–

Now. Agin.

NOON.	**PAN.** *(Sad sad)*
You do have apple!	You do have apple.
I do like apple.	I do like uh apple.

WIN.

Goodgood.

Now. I be foreigner.

NOON.

Aah! Why you always getting to be foreigner?

WIN.

I Win, are furteen.

Noon are tirteen.

Pan are eeleven.

I is so many Engleash.

You is little Engaleash.

Him is bad baby Engleash.

–

You wanting learning or no?

–

Pan.

> **WIN** *in pockets too much garbages*
>
> **WIN** *to pace a foreigner*
>
> *Snap snap* **WIN** *take rando photo, so impress*
>
> **PAN** *bad sly behind* **WIN**
>
> **PAN** *fail two steals for* **WIN** *pockets*
>
> **WIN** *stop, some good twig taps and slaps to* **PAN**

WIN.

Hey-eh, shitty!

I smell you.

–

Noon.

> **PAN** *sad sits*

>   **WIN** *to pace agin and* **NOON** *be sly*
>
>   **NOON** *get in* **WIN** *pocket easy to steal*

NOON.

Ha!   **WIN.**

Aah, goood.

>   **PAN** *clap clap*

NOON.

Now. Foreigner I am.

I like it.

>   **NOON** *she pockets too much garbage*
>
>   **NOON** *to pace to whistle*
>
>   **WIN** *is steal good, but* **PAN** *is no good*

WIN.

I win!

Okay. All us all.

> *Happy music!*
>
> *They run run round try steal each other laughing*
>
> *They smiling and farts*
>
> *Joy music into melodrama!*
>
> **WIN** *and* **NOON** *and* **PAN** *walking up audience asking:*
>
> *"hello-hello" and "money-present?" and "You do have apple? I do like apple."*
>
> *Security with wood stick see childrens and hit chase away them*
>
> **WIN** *is stand in shadow of foreigner*
>
> **WIN** *is reach for steal from foreigner man bag*
>
> *Pause light foreigner turn*
>
> **WIN** *is pose No. 02*
>
> *It is* **THOM**. *He is foreigner dressed like foreigner*

WIN.

Hello-hello?

THOM.

–

Hello.

WIN.

Hello, you do have apple?

THOM.

Sorry. I uh.

–

Sorry.

>   **THOM** *turn back to front*
>
>   **WIN** *try steal from* **THOM** *agin*

>   **THOM** *return*

WIN.

O hello-hello.

Money-present?

THOM.

–

–

>   **THOM** *his pocket he deeply reach*
>
>   *Lint. Loose paper. A gum stick*
>
>   **THOM** *hand gum* **WIN**
>
>   **WIN** *smile put gum to mouth and swallow*

WIN.

(Staring up) Mister you money?

THOM.

I am not "money," I am "Thom."

My name. Thom.

WIN.

Thom.

Thom.

Mister Thom.

Mister Thom Mister Money-Money.

THOM.

No, I wish. Um.

–

Teacher, Thom. I am.

WIN.

Teacha?! Ohh teacha, I know money you have.

Big.

Teacha is money I know you money-money.

THOM.

No I make small money, very small.

Teaching I teach.

Engaleash. I–

WIN.

Engaleash I?? I know:

You. Me. He. Theyym.

Motha. Fatha. Sista. Broda.

–

See. Teacha I know you money.

Please teacha to me I need.

THOM.

Sorry, I.

–

Sorry.

WIN.

–

Small money, okay.

Small money to you teacha biggest money to me.

I no nothing. I no nothing for to have money.

For to feed to Motha. Fatha. Sista.

Small money. Okay?

> **THOM** *reach to pocket deeper and pull from coin*
>
> *Give to* **WIN**

WIN.

(!!)

Ohh, so small money. Yes sir. Small.

I biggest fame-ly.

So many peepul. My motha my fatha.

My sista. My other sista an anotha one.

My brotha. My motha and his sista. My fatha daughta.

My fatha sista daughta and she brotha and–

THOM.

Okay. Okay.

> **THOM** *give* **WIN** *more coin and return round*
>
> **WIN** *eyes bug out*
>
> **WIN** *is winning*
>
> **WIN** *is posing*

WIN.

O hello hello my teacha–

THOM.

I am not–

How old are you?

WIN.

Furteen.

> *(Finger-counting)*

Tirteen?

–

My Engaleash and me is soo poour

please Mister Thom–

THOM.

Thom. No Mister. No sir.

Only Thom, please.

WIN.

Thom. Please.

THOM.

–

How about? Listen.

What if we?
You like Engaleash. I'm a teacher.
What if I teach? One lesson for you.
You stop asking for money. From Me.
And I give you one lesson.

WIN.

–

Engaleash teach to me?

THOM.

You choose.
Asking? Or learning.
If I teach, tomorrow, meet me here.
And only you please, not your big fame-ly.

–

You choose.

> *Light shifty*
>
> **NOON** *poke sickle to garbages looking treasures*
>
> **PAN** *same same but with hand*
>
> **WIN** *wandering thinking looking up*

WIN.

You choose.
You choose.

NOON.

You no have to work?
You big man eh Win? Hehn.

PAN.

Why you look up off?

NOON.

Yeas. Where you brain go?

PAN.

Into clouds

NOON.

Into sky.
Into beauty color.

–

What you see?
Tell to me. I draw it pitcha.

> **NOON** *get chalk and paper*

WIN.

I see nothing I no nothing.

NOON.

You no keep secret from we.
You say. I draw.

WIN.

—

I see...you. And me and she.

In biggest one houses. No, trees houses.

One twos trees. One is you and one is you and one are me.

And apples. So many apples we eating.

And schooling.

And we play eating sleeping and agin until always.

—

The end.

> **PAN** *clap clap and very little cry*
>
> **NOON** *show picture drawing*
>
> **PAN** *take picture drawing*

PAN.

—

We can do.

WIN.

We can do?

PAN.

Here!

It. We can.

WIN.

Here?

We no can do.

NOON.

Eh-eh. There is no nothing we no can do.

Wee? Fame-ly.

> *Wait a minit, who this be coming up in Here?*
>
> *He him foreigner dressed local*
>
> *Children are confusion*
>
> **BACKPACKER** *with camera*
>
> *Snap flash snap to garbage*

BACKPACKER.

(Strangely accent) O. Hello?

> **NOON** *and* **WIN** *and* **PAN** *be silence*
>
> **BACKPACKER** *snap flash snap to garbages*

BACKPACKER.

You.

You speak–

WIN.

Engaleash?

BACKPACKER.

O, Wowuh, you.

Wow.

That's a. Normal.

–

–

I'm Backpacking.

Thought I'd go off the known roads.

You know.

Explore. Adventure.

But. Now I have no idea where I am.

WIN.

Here. You are Here.

NOON.

Why you dress like funny?

BACKPACKER.

O this? This is. Local.

Do I blend in?

> **PAN** *snicker*

WIN.

O yeas.

–

Apple?

You have apple?

> **BACKPACKER** *hand search to fanny pack*

BACKPACKER.

Umm.

Orange?

WIN.

No tank you.

–

Okay.

> **WIN** *take orange to sharing for* **NOON** *and* **PAN** *they eating*
>
> **BACKPACKER** *snap flash take photos no permit*
>
> **NOON** *and* **PAN** *and* **WIN** *stopping eating stare*
>
> **WIN** *is idea*
>
> **WIN** *is pose No. 01*
>
> **BACKPACKER** *sad face and hand inside bag zip zip out more orange give to* **WIN**
>
> **PAN** *pose No. 02,* **NOON** *pose No. 03*
>
> *Snap flash snap* **BACKPACKER** *smile, an award in eyes like stars*
>
> *In pack back* **BACKPACKER** *take from more orange*

BACKPACKER.

Your spirit is. Inspiring.

Especially here amidst all of this. Garbage.

–

I write for a magazine. Abroad.

> *(From pack back, out a Glossy-shiny-weekly)*

We're always looking for images of resilient people in dire circumstance.
I'd like to share these with my editor.
Can I – May I have your verbal consent? To share?

> **WIN** *to take magazine*

> **WIN** *hold out dirty orange to* **BACKPACKER**

WIN.

Share?

BACKPACKER.

(Face) No thanks.
Share these, this.
Your picture.

WIN.

Pictcha? Aah! We have one pictcha, she one is pictcha draw.
Go go, show to him.

> **NOON** *shy, but soon show her pictcha-drawing*

BACKPACKER.

That is.
I dont know what that is.

–

I mean, I like it.

WIN.

I like apple. You do have apple?

BACKPACKER.

No.
What I – I mean I like the you I see here.

> *(He camera)*

The real you.

WIN.

Please and tank you welcome.
I like you I see here.

BACKPACKER.

Your Engaleash is quite impressive.

–

Listen. Do you know – Have you heard
anything about. Um. Ahm. Soldiers?
Around they, well rumored – well, I mean
people have heard I've been told rumors about
plans to cross the border near here. In secret.
Any of that. Familiar?

WIN.

Familyare. Family–are? Yes.

Family are: Motha. Fatha. Brotha. Sista.

See. I know.

BACKPACKER.

You do, you know?

WIN.

Yes I know.

BACKPACKER.

O, I mean O!

I knew it, I heard they were I told my.

Somewhere around, around here, maybe on the move towards?

Something about gas, gas extraction.

Is that what you heard?

–

> *Fanny pack unzip take out apple*
>
> *Holding it forward to* **WIN** *who will take*
>
> **NOON** *and* **PAN** *be trying to sneak* **BACKPACKER** *pack back to steal inside*

BACKPACKER.

I'd like to see it. To take a photo?

For my magazine?

> *(Drop bag unsnap shirt show "Press" vest hiding under)*

See? Can you help me?

> **PAN** *with shortwave radio distract at* **BACKPACKER** *not see* **NOON** *expert thievery*

WIN.

O, help me.

PAN.

(Re: radio) Help you can?

To make work?

WIN.

Yes yes, we need to work?

BACKPACKER.

Work? Sure.

I help you, you help me?

–

–

You need – *(Plug)*

Power.

Do you have power?

> **PAN** *and* **WIN** *mock-imitate*
>
> **NOON** *get so many goodies unsee*

WIN.

You.

You need powah–

BACKPACKER.

No what I need is to find–!

I need to take a photo of combat up close.

So I can show the world, and they can.

See it.

–

Can you help me help you or not?

> *From away away, honk honk!*

BACKPACKER.

That's my driver.

–

–

Well. Well.

Okay I guess.

–

I guess–

WIN.

Bye-bye.

Please to come again.

> *Honk honk!*

BACKPACKER.

Well.

–

Well.

I'll be thinking about you.

And sending you strength. From afar.

> **BACKPACKER**, *Black-Power fist, go gone, bye bye*

WIN.

Thank you, and you?

> **WIN** *waving smiling throwing magazine onto garbages*
>
> *Laughing farts*
>
> *Two smallest battery* **WIN** *from pocket pick up radio them go in it*
>
> *Move dialing, listening*
>
> **PAN** *and* **NOON** *gather count earnings*
>
> *Night fall*

RADIO.

(Recorded) You are listening to Radio Free Radio,

the somewhat, mostly free voice of the People's Resistance.

Today's news is also provided in part by:

The Gary B. and Samantha H. Jankowitz Foundation,
Johnson Family Food Products Incorporated.
The Freedom Partners Prosperity Grassroots Leadership to Reignite Action Fund,
Anonymous. Anonymous. And, Tammy. Just: Tammy.
–

In headlines: on the heels of an historic agreement to resolve the protracted conflict
and bring all parties together in peace accords to discuss compromise – it didn't happen.
Meanwhile, oil prices continue to reach record-breaking highs.
Furthermore, pending reports suggesting several recent facts or rumors have local officials
questioning the future of talk, speech and so-called "news."
–

In other headlines: "Fitted Panties," the number one song in from Abroad,
holds strong for its eighth-straight week,
making the multi-platinum record and its singer Baby Boo a new household name.
And those are the headlines..."

> *Seduce Music coming now: Baby Boo's "Fitted Panties"*

> **WIN** *be slow-dance alone*

> **NOON** *and* **PAN** *falling to sleeping*

BABY BOO & SINGERS. *(Through radio)*
LAY ON THEM STARS
LOOK AT THE GIRL YOU SEE
HERE IN YOUR ARMS
I'LL SHOW YOU MY CHAR-I-TEE
OOOO YOUR EYES-SUH
GET ME SOOOO WET
ITS RAINY RAIN DOWN IN MY PANTS
CAN'T WAIT TO

MAKE YOU SWEAT
INSIDE A YOUR
FITTED PANTIES
THEY SO FITTED
THEM FITTED PANTIES
YEAH YE-AH YEA...

> *Do we see back of* **BABY BOO** *in shadow/silhouette?*

BABY BOO.
(Spoken, recording) Yeah baby
This is a public service announcement
Ooowwawawa
Our love is so...unspecified
But before I finish, let me just say
I did not come here to show out
Did not come here to impress you
Because to tell you the truth when I leave here I'm gone girl
And I don't care what you think about me, but just remember
When it hits the fan baby, whether it's next year, ten years

You're never gonna be able to say
That they lied to you Jack

> *Awaking as daydream is* **WIN**
> *Lighty light*

THOM.
...Jack?
Jack?

WIN.
(Soup sip slurp)

THOM.
And?

WIN.
And Hill want up–

THOM.
Jill.

WIN.
Jill. Want up. A hill.
To catched. A pail. Af wata.

THOM.
Close.

WIN.
Jack fall down, broke her crown–

THOM.
Her?
Is Jack a girl?

WIN.
–
Broke. Him crown.
Jill came tumble afta.

THOM.
Great. Very good.

WIN.
Tank you tank you.

THOM.
Th. Thank.

WIN.
Th. Thank.

THOM.
Good.

WIN.
Have good teacha.

THOM.
I have. A good. Teacher.

WIN.

I have. A good. Teacher.

THOM.

Yes. True.

–

> *(Smiles)*

I have a good student.

–

Well.

Well I must be leaving.

WIN.

Please and thank you come agin?

> *(Slurp)*

Teach to me?

THOM.

–

You like the teaching?

Well.

–

I guess.

Maybe.

WIN.

Please to me teacher??

–

I have present you?

> **WIN** *deep reach pockets*
> *Pull out small rock-present*

THOM.

Thank you?

I'm.

It's.

Thank you.

–

Ahh, I have.

A present for you.

> *Now,* **THOM** *reach search in he bag take out dry tea one*

WIN.

Money present?!

THOM.

No. Here.

There.

WIN.

What it?

THOM.

Tea.

From where I'm from. From home.

It's. I brought it with me. When I moved. Here.

I carry it. To remind –.

Helps my concentration a little tea.

Keeps me. Organized.

Maybe it can help you too. With.

It is very good. Strong. See?

Here. My gift.

To you.

> **WIN** *is dreamy eyes*
>
> *Lights shifty*
>
> **WIN** *walking back at dump site*
>
> **WIN** *play with teabag*
>
> **PAN** *open mouth sleep sleepy snore on garbages*
>
> **NOON** *waiting patient*

WIN.

Good. Strong. See?

> *See* **NOON**, *stash teabag pocket*

WIN.

Hey.

NOON.

Hey.

–

Where you was go?

WIN.

I go... *(Around-ish)*

NOON.

I waiting.

WIN.

You can go too.

Wherever you want.

NOON.

No. We cannot leave to him?

PAN.

(Nicely dream) Mm mm manggooo.

WIN.

Him okay.

Pan Pan? You okay?

NOON.

Now you can waiting.

Why I can go.

For toilet.

> **NOON** *is take paper, go bye toilet*
>
> **WIN** *is boring sitting looking tea packet*
>
> **PAN** *sleepsnore*
>
> **W.H.O.** *is coming Here?*
> *Look deeply bedraggled nurse and so bureaucracy*
> *Face-mask over mouth making strange noise*

W.H.O.

(*Mumble-meh*) (*Move mask*) Pardon.

WIN.

Who, you?

W.H.O.

Why yes.

Sorry to keep you waiting.

WIN.

Waiting? For what?

W.H.O.

(*Point emblem*) Whooo. Double-you ach O?

WIN.

–

You?

W.H.O.

No. Yes. Officially I'm unofficial.

On contract – not full-time, not yet. But soon.

Thanks to the promise of war, there will be a lot more work to do around Here.

I can almost smell those benefits: pension, paid leave, diplomatic immunity.

Once I've reached my quota that is, and nearly there.

Fingers-crossed. Shall we begin?

–

The survey?

WIN.

The what?

> **WIN** *to follow and imitate moments*

W.H.O.

The Whhoo.

You receive our letter?

We sent letter via post.

It said we would be by to make a survey.

WIN.

(?)

> **W.H.O.** *to garbages searching*

W.H.O.

Looks like – like – Here it is. Yes.

See:

"We're coming."

WIN *try read*

W.H.O.

Let's get started – time is of the essence.

I'll just need a few quotes for my quota.

I'm paid by the letter not the hour.

Can you state your name for record?

WIN.

My name?

W.H.O.

For record.

WIN.

I am.

I am–

W.H.O.

"I Am"? Excellent.

And I-am, how old are you?

WIN.

Tirteen?

W.H.O.

Hm.

–

Eee-leven.

And I-am, what is your address here?

WIN.

Here? We are Here.

W.H.O.

Yes here? But here is?

WIN.

Here is Here.

W.H.O.

Here is here?

–

Ahh-k.

You know, I get it. Resistance to change.

Change, it can be good though.

Take for examples: me. I don't want to be here.

I want to change to be somewhere else. Anywhere!

But especially in our air-conditioned office in the setee.

Behind a nice desk, near the coffee makings machines.

Yet, on the ground, is where I must be.

Before I can move up and out.

WIN.

I can move up and out.

W.H.O.

Yes, You, Can. And: the sooner the better.

Now. To the survey?

–

Oof. I forget. First, they make me to read this disclaimer.

    (Reading)

'Hem. As you probably do not know, the W.H.O. is the preeminent global body
on matters regarding the health of our public wealth.
We practice harm reduction and attraction,
and I'm here today on behalf of all multilaterals and not only us.
This survey is intended to collect info, micro and meta-data
on statusless individuals such as you living in, at, and around – Here.
Those data will then be manipulated into statistics
which will then be aggregated and used to advocate for-profit
which will then be activated to ensure that you the interest-bearing patient
which will then be possibly likely plagued by debt or some serious infectious diseases
which will then be crawling away inside of your flesh, and our mutual fund
which will then be mutant and threatening to spread across the global
which will then be frightened of and stigmatizing toward you for your low credit rating
which will then be mandated by shareholders to gather more data about the data
which will then be put into another report written to preempt the disinvestment campaign
which will then be given to the assistant of the secretary of the general secretary
who will once again be a useless nobody from an unknown place you can't even pronounce
who will then be forced into making various, curated quotes based on quotas from my original
report but not about the bits that matter. Most of that will be immediately, post-delivery, all but
buried and forgotten about.
Clear?

WIN.

–

No.

W.H.O.

Great.
Now if you could please to sign?

    WIN *try at reading*

W.H.O.

Please to sign.
There.

    WIN *mark*

W.H.O.

And here.

    WIN *mark*

W.H.O.
And here.

> **WIN** *mark*

W.H.O.
And here.

> **WIN** *mark*

W.H.O.
And here.

> **WIN** *mark*

W.H.O.
And here.

> **WIN** *mark*

W.H.O.
And here and here.
And there.
–
Oh, you missed –

> **WIN** *marks*

W.H.O.
Finnish.
Now, if you don't mind –

> **W.H.O.** *from somewhere pull out biggest pointy needle squirt squirt*

W.H.O.
I'd like to inoculate you.

> **WIN** *eyes bug out*

W.H.O.
Oh don't worry. It's complementary.

> **WIN** *is backing* **W.H.O.** *is toward*

WIN.
I have to go toilet!

> **WIN** *race race hide away*
> **W.H.O.** *wait*
> **W.H.O.** *walk round to survey waiting*

WIN.
(*Loud*) I'm going now.
–
I'm leaving you several pharmaceutical samples.

> *From big-bag* **W.H.O.** *take pill bottle*
> *And pill bottle*
> *And pill bottle*

And pill bottles

And wow so many drugs from that bag

And all it go near somewhere

W.H.O. *look around to dispose needles*

W.H.O. *throw needles on garbages near* **PAN**

W.H.O. *waving leaving going goodbyeing*

WIN *pop up head near garbages*

WIN *see no* **W.H.O.** *so "whew" and crip walk return*

PAN *snort to awake and wipe at eyes*

Look about **PAN** *and pick up needle surprise*

WIN *come round mistake* **PAN** *with needle for* **W.H.O.** *scare*

WIN.

(Scream)

PAN.

(Scream)

WIN *and* **PAN** *relief*

WIN *take needle from* **PAN** *and throw away*

NOON *arrive empty toilet roll*

NOON.

Hey.

PAN & WIN.

(Scream)

NOON.

–

No more paper.

(See pills bottle so many)

What this is?

NOON *grab bottle*

NOON *shake shake*

WIN *grab new bottle shake*

WIN *and* **NOON** *shake*

WIN *and* **NOON** *shake*

They rhythm make

WIN & NOON.

Eh-ehhh! Woot-woot!

PAN *is smile*

PAN *is hand-waving in air like he just don't care*

PAN *is crip walk taking bottle shaking*

Light shifty and **PAN** *and* **NOON** *stay make music throughout*

WIN is dreamy eyes curious

A beauty sky in starry night

THOM *enter sit to besides to* **WIN** *with teacup*

THOM *hand tea cup for* **WIN** *drinking*

THOM *from bag take big-size box tea gift to* **WIN**

Smiling and star-gaze be flash beauty

Them watching them stars

WIN *reach over and holding* **THOM** *hand*

THOM *see hands*

Light another way, back to dump site

Rain sounds hitting metal and plastics

NOON *and* **PAN** *are boring*

NOON *waiting impatient*

PAN *slow shake pill bottle*

PAN.
Rainy season.

NOON.
–

It always rainy season.

> **PAN** *is shake pill bottle*
> **PAN** *is surprise open pill bottle looking inside it*
> **PAN** *pulling out colorful pill and smile*

PAN.
Candy?

(Eating)

Mmm.
Mmmm candiee?!

NOON. That is no candy.

> **WIN** *appear a little wet tarp overhead*

NOON.
–

Where you were?

WIN.
Meeting to my friend

NOON.
You who friend?

WIN.
I do have outside friend.

–

Here. I bringing this one.

It soopah. Strong.

> **WIN** *smile and open tea box*

> **WIN** *take out tea and put in garbage cup*

> **WIN** *catch rain and mixing water with tea to drink*

> *Tea is passing around and drinking*
> **PAN** *is finally*
> *Unsee,* **PAN** *put color pill in teacup and drink it*
> **PAN** *smile and eyes blinky*

> *Everyone is boring*
> *Rain stop sky clearly*
> *Everyone is smile ready to play*

> *Surprise surprise face-painted* **MIME** *is enter*
> *Another* **CLOWN** *is come Here carry biggest balloons!*
> *Both they perform tiny routine*
> **PAN** *and* **WIN** *and* **NOON** *watch too frighten, not happy*

> *Routine is finish in shocking poses*
> **CLOWN** *and* **MIME** *holding waiting hoping desperate applause*
> *No fanfare*
> **PAN** *exit screaming*

CLOWN.
Oh little boy, dont cry. It's going to be alright.
Let us entertain you.
We're here in this savage land to encourage laughter.
Also, we hope to find time to tour your beautiful, decaying boondocks.
You might call it: a work-cation. Killing two birds with one stone, eh??
It's a Win-Win.

NOON.
Him, he is Win-Win.
Me, I Noon.
Who you?
This you outside friend?

WIN.
(Head shake)

CLOWN.
We are from Clowns Across Bounds.
We've come to bring joy into your sad little lives.
Here. This is our mission statement.

> **MIME** *and poof appear a papers*

WIN.
O? Hello-hello.
You have apple?

You have money-present? You money-money?

CLOWN.

Sorry.

We're a nonprofit organization.

–

Achew! Bless me.

(Clears throat)

MIME.

(Clears throat)

CLOWN.

Parched.

–

May I have a sip of your water?

WIN.

Watah? What?

Tea this be. Not watah.

CLOWN.

Tea? Even better!

I have a cold.

>   **CLOWN** *take teacup no permit and* **MIME** *make invisible teacup*
>   *They drink*
>   **CLOWN** *and* **MIME** *look each other eyes bug out*

CLOWN.

O m–my.

God

–

>   *(Shaky shake)*

O this – this tea is. Orgasmic.

–

What secret foreign spice.

What is it?

What is in here?

WIN.

What in what in where?

CLOWN.

In Here!

I must know.

WIN.

You want?

–

You. Have money-present?

>   **MIME** *pull out paper money lots and hand over*
>   **NOON** *and* **WIN** *bug-out eyes counting*

Devil music
Mumble-mumble from afar
NOON *and* **WIN** *be bad fanfare!*

NOON.

We hide!   **WIN.**

                                                  We must to hide now!

NOON *and* **WIN** *hide disappear behind garbages*

CLOWN *and* **MIME** *think game so camo hide in nearby trashes*

Now arriving is **MILITIA**

MILITIA *look like police-army-gangsta-local*

MILITIA *carry machete and gun and liquor drinking a lot*

MILITIA.

(Mumble-mumble) Pets.
My pupppppetttsss!
Where you I find?
–
Hide and seek eh?
I find. You no can hide from me.
Militia.
Join to us. We, all-volunteer.
Serve. Protect, Tha national guard.
We. Guard tha nationalism.
–

Drunk **MILITIA** *pee-pee near* **MIME**

Bad singing

MILITIA.

OoOoOo your eyes
Get me soooo wet
Rainy rain in pantalon
Cant wait to make you – Recruits!
Where you at you??
–
I find is no good.
You come to me, is good.

CLOWN *sneeze*

MILITIA *see* **CLOWN**

CLOWN *breaking character to hold out hand toward that* **MILITIA**

CLOWN.

Bless me!
Hello friend.
We're from Clowns Across Bounds.
We've come to bring your community joy and laughter

despite your –

>   **MILITIA** *shoot* **CLOWN** *in face*

>   **CLOWN** *on the ground dead and bleeding*

>   *Long quiet*

>   *Very slow* **MIME** *trying escaping*

>   **MILITIA** *see and shoot* **MIME** *in the leg*

>   **MIME** *mimes a scream*

MILITIA.
Pets.
You friends is dying.
Everywhere. Everyone are dying.

>   *Quiet*

MILITIA.
Patriots?
Good pay we give. 401k??

–

Next I come you join.
You no can choose.

>   **MILITIA** *pick up limp body that* **MIME**

>   **MILITIA** *drag that limp body*

>   **MILITIA** *go away away*

>   **WIN** *and* **NOON** *appear agin*

>   *Stare they at that dead body* **CLOWN**

>   *Pop-kill those balloons* **WIN**, *one by one*

>   *They together bury* **CLOWN** *body under garbages, no fanfare*

>   *They look at lots money and teacup*

>   *A idea!*

>   *Happy Music!*

>   **NOON** *draw and post sign: "Teashop"*

>   **PAN** *appear and* **WIN** *setup teashop*

>   *Most all shop stuffs is recycle from garbages, but cleanish*

>   *Small table is one*

>   *Three chairs is two*

>   *All is small chairs like a kid furniture*

>   *Teapot of metal, broken cups, and stuffs*

>   **PAN** *cutting mango*

>   **NOON** *be reluctant waitress*

>   **WIN** *and* **THOM** *and* **CIGARETTE MAN** *sit at table*

>   *At table all is creepy quiet and smiles*

Some shifty hands and shifty eyes
CIGARETTE MAN *is smoke-smokey*
He been talking soooo much
WIN *is cigarette fake-smoking*

CIGARETTE MAN.

(Cough-clear throat) Uncertainty–?–the enemy of investment.

What's your value? Dont be disposable.

Time is money money is honey, honey is runny, sticky, sweet.

WIN.

–

Yeas?

CIGARETTE MAN.

Functionality. Company?

T'will be very value when this violent warfare business is done.

And people need new things to do. With their hands.

> *(Funny-waving-hands)*

You know I mean?

WIN.

O yeeaas.

–

Noon?

> **WIN** *mimic funny hands, beckon* **NOON** *come to fan to* **CIGARETTE MAN**

CIGARETTE MAN.

(To **WIN***)* Do you have mind for business, Jack?

THOM.

He is quite resourceful. Very take-charge. In fact–

CIGARETTE MAN.

So small, I see.

WIN.

Yeas, small but big. I see: Bizness. Teashop, ownah is we–

CIGARETTE MAN.

Human capital. Everybody's eyeballing extractives.

People comes, and everything goes.

They come, say: where do we go to drill baby drill?

Natural gas–?–Oh yes.

Who moved my cheese??

I did.

Decades ago, I moved Here from Abroad.

To play hard and work less.

Even with little, I live like king.

Here. I win.

WIN.

Here. I, Win.

CIGARETTE MAN.

Ah, so we speak the same language.

>*(To* **THOM***)*

Such a good student.

WIN.

Tank you.

THOM.

Th. Thank you.

WIN.

Th. Thank you.

>*(To* **PAN***)*

Mango?!

>**PAN** *bring that mango*

CIGARETTE MAN.

(To **PAN***)* Oh who is this little gas pump?

WIN.

He? Him is one from Here.

Like we. Us.

See, Him is tea-make.

Her is wait-wait.

I is welcome.

NOON.

No, am I is welcome.

WIN.

No. You is wait-wait.

CIGARETTE MAN.

(To **PAN***)* Do you speak Engaleash?

PAN.

Yes. I do like apple.

CIGARETTE MAN.

Impressive.

PAN.

(To **WIN***)* I have good teacha.

WIN.

(To **PAN***)* I have. A good. Teach-er.

CIGARETTE MAN.

So many teachers. A noble profession, yes. But?

Some people teach, and some people do: Business.

I like to have things to do.

THOM.

(Defensive) I have things to do.

– *(Stands)*

I mean. My students don't teach themselves.

Glad I could connect you.

Always happy to help.

> (*To* **CIGARETTE MAN**, *re:* **WIN**)

He's a small businessman in the making.

> **WIN** *take* **THOM** *aside*

> **NOON** *try sly stealing from* **CIGARETTE MAN**

WIN.

Mister Thom, he will invest?

In our teashop?

THOM.

I'm sure it will all work out.

See you soon?

PAN.

(Wave to **THOM***)* Thank you

NOON.

Welcome.

> **CIGARETTE MAN** *produce tiny candy*

CIGARETTE MAN.

(To **PAN***)* Care for a candy?

NOON.

He should no have candy no.

WIN.

He can have you give.

CIGARETTE MAN.

Listen you two, competitive? I like it.

Fffiiiight! Competition drives innovation.

And I'm a fan of, especially competitive tickling.

You know? Here, let me show it you.

> *(Beckon to* **PAN**, *then steal tickle no permit)*

–

You lose! Now, do me.

> **PAN** *sad-smile*

> **CIGARETTE MAN** *tickles* **PAN** *agin*

CIGARETTE MAN.

Too slow – I win.

> *Cough-cough.*

PAN.

(Re: **WIN***)* Him. He is Win.

CIGARETTE MAN.

(To **NOON***)* You. Care to play??

NOON.

(Bug eyes and shaking head "no")

WIN.

(To **CIGARETTE MAN**) But first, you can to try our tea?

CIGARETTE MAN.

Gladly.

>   (Take tea slow staring **PAN**)

>   (Drinking teaing staring)

Yum.

–

Yum yum.

WIN.

Yes? Invest yumm?

CIGARETTE MAN.

Yes yum.

Yyyyyum.

>   **CIGARETTE MAN** sticking finger in glass and him licking licking

>   **NOON** trying stealing, but **WIN** shoo-shoo

CIGARETTE MAN.

Why is it so yum?

WIN.

We is strong. Our tea.

Soopah power.

You...money?

CIGARETTE MAN.

Owh.

I feel...ready to play.

Awwhh. Awhwhwow.

Mmmm.

>   (Sigh)

I know all I need to know.

>   (Stand-leaving)

NOON.

Wait! Wait you will to invest??

CIGARETTE MAN.

You are functional. You are selling.

They will buy.

I tell my friends, all.

Of your dolicious tea.

And company.

>   **CIGARETTE MAN** baby-waving away bye bye gone

NOON.

Nmm. Him breath is too smelly.

>   **NOON** fart-laughing to **PAN**

NOON.

(Hold up theft item) Look what I steal it!

PAN.

Yay, look! What it?

WIN.

Noon, we is bizness now, we no to steal.

NOON.

Who no to steal? Him leave money-present??

I get it.

WIN.

You is confus-ed.

NOON.

I is no confus-ed.

And him be funny-acting foreigner.

WIN.

All foreigner be funny.

NOON.

That no mean I have to like to them.

ACTRESS.

Ahem.

PAN.

Psst!

> *Now this lady* **ACTRESS** *come in nobody notice*
>
> **ACTRESS** *is big hat and sunglass*
>
> **ASSISTANT-GUARD**, *a little mean-face follow close her behind*

WIN.

(To **NOON***)* You no nothing. We must to bizness.

PAN.

Psst!

WIN.

O Miss! A nice one lady.

You mostly wel–

ACTRESS.

Ssshhh!

WIN.

O. Kay.

> *(Whispa)*

Welcome.

> **WIN** *wonder walk to garbages rummage for find magazine*
>
> **PAN** *secret eating pills*
>
> *Do he look a little very much sicker than we saw before? He do*

NOON.

(To **ACTRESS***)* How you know our teashop?

We is new.

ACTRESS.

Word travels fast, I know things.

Once a place like this opens I aim to beat the crowds.

I'm in. I know.

NOON.

You, Know.

I, welcome.

ACTRESS.

O, hello, "Welcome." What a cute local name.

Listen – is it true?

I've heard: people EAT the cats here.

NOON.

–

No, we no eat cats.

ACTRESS.

H! Ha! Then where are they?

WIN.

(*Returning*) Hallo-hello agin.

Every okay here? You have question?

I am ownahship. Of teashop, I am ownahship

NOON.

You no ownahship, we is all co-operate in Here

WIN.

(*Whispa*) Someone need to take charge.

You is dumb-dumb Engaleash, Him is helpless baby Engaleash.

I am take charge.

ACTRESS.

You take charge??

Awh! Ernesto?!

> **ASSISTANT-GUARD** *bring give plastic credit to* **ACTRESS**
>
> **ACTRESS** *shoo-shoo* **ASSISTANT-GUARD**, *he back away*
>
> **WIN** *give plastic credit to* **NOON** *and shoo-shoo her away*
>
> **NOON** *take offense and plastic credit confuse*

ACTRESS.

(*After* **NOON**) Keep the tab open.

> **WIN** *is star-eyes flip through magazine*

WIN.

Does I know you?

> (*Magazine point*)

Looking is similar.

ACTRESS.

But in these glasses?

–
–

>*(Mouthing: Yes. It's. Me!)*

–

>*(Yessss!)*

WIN.
O my got – O you are in this pitcha-book!!

ACTRESS.
Yes!! Sshh! We're being followed
everywhere.
I'm here on a goodwill mission. We've absconded
through a backdoor of our hotel in order to evade the paparazzi.
Just a quick expedition, to witness local life without all of the
advancing. Maybe even buy a trinket or two, hm?
Support your local economy. Invest in real people.

WIN.
Invest??

>*(To **NOON**)*

Cushion-a!

>**NOON** *rummage through garbages to find pillow*

ACTRESS.
Here.
Off the map, away from the maddening crowds.

>**NOON** *bring cushion for* **WIN**

>**WIN** *push cushion under* **ACTRESS**

ACTRESS.
Th–thank you.

>**WIN** *star* **ACTRESS**

WIN.
Th. Thank you.
You beauty-filled.

ACTRESS.
O, well.

>*(To **NOON**)*

You're: Welcome.
You like...the outfit I wore?

WIN.
I, War?
You like war?? We can show.
I know.
We give what you want. You no can see War
but you will.

You see what you want, we can give.

We was take but now we give,

and big.

We is disaster touring company.

We too is pictcha-drawing company.

We too is for-profit teaching Engaleash company.

We too many many drugs you can buy for cheap-cheap company.

But I know you want to see is war, right?

You foreigner all same so interest to see fighting and I can show.

NOON.

For money-present?

ACTRESS.

No!

I'm off the humanitarian clock. No more, the

remnant of fighting, over natural resources? The gas?

I need a break. I cannot see another concave stomach, not today.

Even I used to have one – on the runways of Pair-ee.

(Sad memory)

That was ages ago.

Woe. No more remnant of war for me.

> **ACTRESS** *become lip quiver emotion*

WIN.

–

You want tea?

We have tea?

> **ACTRESS** *recover and flip through magazine pages*

ACTRESS.

Why not? One tea.

Then back. To Goodwill Ambassadoring.

> **WIN** *is shoo-shoo to* **NOON,** *but she no get up*

WIN.

Tea-la?!

(To **ACTRESS***)*

Our tea here is soopah.

We are soopah powah tea!

Trust I.

It very dolicious.

ACTRESS.

Yes, well.

I'll be the judge of that.

–

I am, you know. A judge. On, The Judge of That.

It's a reality competition. On cable – have you seen it?

Do you get cable? Here?

> *(Magazine)*

Here see that's me in the middle there. I'm the nice one.

> *(Sigh)*

It's time I move out of reality.

Shake up my career. Expand horizons.

Does your life ever feel like a series of cameos? Mine does.

My resume – bit part after bit part.

But I'm ready to break out of the ensemble, make a name for myself.

I want to be an acTOR not an acTRESS.

Why can't I have a role with a saucy accent?

(Bad British) Ello Guvnah??

> *(To **WIN**, **NOON**)*

Life is as short as you are. And underdeveloped.

But I need a long-term strategy.

–

Maybe I'll quit. Give up my gifts. Move Here. Open a coffeeshop?

I could couldn't I? I could stay for – minutes. Hours even.

Here are none of the distractions of real life.

> *(Long sigh)*

–

I'm bored.

WIN.

*(To **NOON** clap clap)* Tea-la!

> **NOON** *reluctant get up*

> **NOON** *go over to that **PAN** who is no make tea*

WIN.

Sorry for you long waiting.

ACTRESS.

–

(Bad melodrama) Everybody be uh waitin'. Everybody be uh wanton.

But not everybody be uh gettin'.

–

That's a line. From a play I was in.

My character, the older ingenue, was living in squalor much like this.

And boy, did she have some wisdoms.

They don't write roles like that anymore.

Parts where you really get to ACTT.

> *Her small spittle hit to **WIN***

> **ACTRESS** *wonder*

ACTRESS.

Meow?

Where are they then? Your cats??

        ACTRESS *finally see that stiff-standing, high-getting* **PAN**

ACTRESS.

Oo – What is this?

My. Look what – what is this?

WIN.

What what is?

ACTRESS.

This. Such an exquisite puppet.

And lifelike. Did you find it in the garbage?

O my god, it blinks! Is it electric? Is it gas?!

I know things. This puppet is antique. I've an eye.

Look at the greying features, that sad little cracked-out mouth.

Is it for sale?

O, I simply must have it – how much for it?

WIN.

How much what it?

ACTRESS.

It, I simply must.

NOON.

Him? Sale he is not for.

ACTRESS.

You, I admire your moxie. Go to, lean in!

You've got agency, and I've got an agent too.

He said: If they ever call you a bitch, just own it.

Can't I own it? If it's not for sale than what is it??

You were probably about to throw it out anyway.

Put it on my tab Drinks on the house – how much?

WIN.

How. Much?

NOON.

Sale he is not for!

PAN.

What is happening?

ACTRESS.

(Yelp) And it speaks!

O, O, I must have it. Ernesto?!

NOON.

No!

        NOON *pointing* **PAN** *go he shuffle away*

ACTRESS.

(To **NOON***)* I don't mean to pathologize you, but. May I?

Why are you bitter and being so loudly?

Your friend is well-spoken. While your Engaleash?

You should be nicer.

Open the resonators, work your enunciation.

Now because I'm an acTOR and I came to help I can assist you with this?

'Hem.

Hooow Nooww Brownn Cowww.

NOON.

Brownn coww?!

ACTRESS.

Good.

Now say that seven times fast, throughout the day, and

people will learn to love you.

> **NOON** *back-away fake smile and so many bows*

NOON.

–

Thank you, Miss.

> **NOON** *now mixing stirring teaing and in put two whole bottle pills secret*

ACTRESS.

Now see See there. I love that about your people, Welcome.

Good listeners, Impressionable. Able to change in an instant.

Here is full of distress and surprises – reminds me of me.

I'm not religious, but I'm spiritual. And you have that belief,

what's that thing – You know, it's – O – what is? ...Merit?

Merit. To carry you into the afterlife. The act of giving and good deeds.

That. Is noble.

> **NOON** *pouring teaing bringing one cup over*
>
> **WIN** *try to take from but* **NOON** *refuse*

NOON.

(Fake) Noval? I no know. What it mean, noval?

ACTRESS.

Noble. Nooble. It's like –

'hem.

> *(Bad melodrama definition with hands outreach and more)*

Like that.

WIN.

(Re: tea) Finely.

NOON.

Yes, Finely.

ACTRESS.

This has been fun, hasn't it?

My being here with you? Teaching you how to act.

Acting is delightful.

It's fun to escape the pain of the present. Even if only

for a moment.

To hideaway in a fake foreign land.
To pretend we're not exactly where we are. Here.
To ignore the truth of what's happening.
Ignorance makes the pill of reality easier to swallow.
There's always a War. Even here at home.
Everything is disposable.

>   *(Pick-up-chug tea)*

Wow, that is – that's tea?! It tastes like. I don't even know.
–
Like an epidemic.

>   *(Mouth begin slowly droopy)*
>
>   *(Spittle droppings)*
>
>   *(She tongue-voice sound strangely anesthetized)*

I feel...wonderful.

>   *(She snap out it but tongue-voice still wagging)*
>
>   *(She grab up purse and dig through with fever)*

Pack up that tea, I'll take it! Shipped to this address. Abroad.
Are you looking to export? Franchise??
I want a majority stake, eighty-twenty.

WIN.
–

ACTRESS.
Okay seventy-thirty.

WIN.
Well. I – we–

ACTRESS.
Sixty-forty but I want a guaranteed equity bond.

WIN.
I um–

ACTRESS.
Fifty-fifty and throw in the puppet.

NOON.
No, I say it him is no for–!
Get out!

ACTRESS.
You can't talk to me like that.
I'm a patron. I'm patronizing you.

NOON.
Out!

ACTRESS.
Not until I am satisfied.

NOON.
You satisfy our tea?! Okay.

Me give you all the tea you want it.

>**NOON** *go grab hot water pot*
>
>*She make to throw at* **ACTRESS**

ACTRESS.

(Short yelp) No we will go. I have important meetings.
Contracts to sign. Babies to kiss
Peace deals to negotiate.

>*(Leaving, turning)*
>
>*(Give card to* **WIN***)*

If you're ever in Abroad. Call me.

>*(Exit)*

WIN.

Noon! What mattah you?
She is paying to us money.

NOON.

She make fun me, my Engaleash?
You too??

WIN.

You no nothing You bad luck for bizness

NOON.

H!! Here?
I am steal is my bizness, and I am good it.
I am play and recreate is my bizness.
I am babysit and I enjoy mango.
You want inviting teashop say "hello foreigner"?
You so being admire to them. Calling: "you beauty-filled."
You fetish foreigner.
Who was last one you take money to steal from, hm?
You forget how? You is lazy now.

>**WIN** *slap* **NOON**, *she stunning*
>
>**NOON** *hold her own face in hand*
>
>*Pause*

ANNOUNCER.

(Recorded) Welcome back to The Angel Cable Channel.
You are watching "Concert For A Cure to the Poverty and World Peace also Africa."
And now, the star of our show,
multi-platinum recording artist: Baby Boo!

>*Orchestral music! Fanfare!*
>
>*Light up* **BABY BOO** *in foreground*
>
>*He in tuxedo and ball-cap*
>
>*He is number one singer of song*

BABY BOO.

LAY ON THEM STARS
LOOK AT THE GIRL YOU SEE
HERE IN MY ARMS
I'LL SHOW YOU MY CHAR-I-TEE
OOOOOO YOUR EYES
GET ME SOOOO WET
ITS RAINY RAIN DOWN IN MY PANTS
CANT WAIT TO MAKE YOU
CANT WAIT TO MAKE YOU
SWEEAATT
INSIDE A YOUR

> *Light up* **GOSPEL CHOIR** *in background*
>
> *They so clap soul and ooo's aahh's and ad-libs*

BABY BOO & GOSPEL CHOIR.

FITTED PANTIES
THEY SO FITTED
SO SO TIGHT
THEM FITTED PANTIES
YEAH YE-AH YEAS...

BABY BOO.

This is a public service announcement
Our love is so unspecified
But before I finish, let me just say
I did not come here to show out
Did not come here to impress you
And I don't care what you think about me
but just remember –

> *Quiet*
>
> **PAN** *alone in spotlight we see*
>
> **PAN** *is sickly & unsure & hopeful*
>
> *He is, no pose*
>
> *Him eat swallow two colorful pill*
>
> *Bomb bomb*
>
> *Lights*
>
> *Go*
>
> *All gone now cept* **NOON** *and* **WIN** *and* **PAN** *as before, no fanfare*
>
> **NOON** *hold her face*
>
> *She cry*
>
> *She run run away*
>
> **WIN** *clean up around*

PAN.

Win.

Win.

WIN.

What?

PAN.

We is fame-ly we.

WIN.

Are we?

PAN.

–

We is fame-ly we.

She are we.

WIN.

We is bizness.

To making money we are.

PAN.

We making fame-ly and she is–

WIN.

She is losing.

No money can come if money is go.

–

She want. She can learning?

Or she can go.

> **NOON** *appear on other side*
>
> *In dirt,* **NOON** *to draw line with sickle*
>
> **NOON** *hold in other hand pictcha-drawing*

NOON.

Bye bye!

PAN.

Yay! She back

NOON.

(*To* **WIN**) My mark.

WIN.

What that?

NOON.

(*To* **WIN**) My new pictcha-draw.

My red line.

You ovah there. Me ovah here. Now to on and all.

This my red line. Keep away.

WIN.

–

Okay.

NOON.

–

You no come to here.

No for school teaching.

No for nothing, I no have nothing you.

WIN.

Okay.

NOON.

Pan! Come come here.

> **PAN** *stiff stone*

NOON.

Come here come!

> **PAN** *slow move*

WIN.

Eh-ehe-eh.

> **PAN** *be stone stiff then, backwards walk*

NOON.

Pan you come I watch.

WIN.

Pan my friend.

Not you friend.

NOON.

Pan my // friend.

WIN.

Nonot.

NOON.

Pan my // friend.

WIN.

Nono, no friend.

He is over here.

> **NOON** *to cry stop quick*
>
> *Hand to sickle hard*

NOON.

No friend. You and you

No friend.

You come over to line.

You no friend.

> *Quiet*
>
> **WIN** *turn round*
>
> **WIN** *turn* **PAN** *round they back to* **NOON**
>
> *Local man of dump people appear*
>
> *Or is it* **CIGARETTE SMOKER** *so sicker sunk face?*
>
> *He skulk no seen*

WIN.

Fine.

Peepul come and peepul go.

Go.

I no mind.

> *Skulk man grab to* **NOON** *from behind her*
>
> *Muffled screams of* **NOON**
>
> **WIN** *and* **PAN** *notice not*

WIN.

Whatwhat??

You say, I cant to hear to you.

You say some word?

Your Engaleash is too bad no understand, hh.

> **NOON** *be assaulted by strange man*
>
> *Man put hand to* **NOON** *mouth*
>
> **PAN** *try to turn but* **WIN** *return*
>
> *They no notice*

WIN.

Is it the line?

What about it?

You draw it.

I no draw, hh.

What that?

> *Man draggings to* **NOON**
>
> **NOON** *all kicks and muffled mouths*
>
> **NOON** *drop pictcha-draw where she stood*
>
> *Now she away away gone*

PAN.

(Smiling) Okay enough. We sorry.

> **PAN** *turnround and* **NOON** *not seen to be*
>
> **PAN** *go pick up pictha-drawing*

PAN.

Noon? Noon?

  Dark

  Light

  Blacklight?

  A sterile place

  A place of sterility

  Perhaps, a theater

  A pristine theater

  Florescents. Febreze

  The smell of fresh paint

  WIN and PAN are dolled-up

  They look in disguise

  They stand staring at the spectators

  They stand. WIN squirms

  They stand

WIN.
They have no answer.
They do not talk back.

PAN.
Sssh.

WIN.
I leave.

PAN.
No, we must together.

   WIN *walks toward another wall and stops*

   WIN *turns around to see if* **PAN** *is following*

   PAN *continues staring out*

   WIN *returns*

WIN.
She leave us, not us leave her.
Why we in setee–

PAN.
Sshh.

WIN.
What if we get catched–

PAN.
We wont.

   A window in a wall where there wasn't one before

   WIN *and* **PAN** *stiffen. From inside the window:*

VOICE.
Which form?

WIN & PAN.

   –

VOICE.

   Which form?

   –

   Alpha, Beta, Omega?

PAN.

   Ahm–

       The window disappears down like a guillotine

WIN.

   O shit, I will go.

PAN.

   No.

WIN.

   I will.

   They will eat us.

PAN.

   No.

WIN.

   She leave us, so I leave her.

       The window opens. Cigarette smoke rises from it

VOICE.

   Which form?

PAN.

   Ahm. We sir – no have I – ahm. Form.

VOICE.

   Nonsense.

   Next!

   –

       PAN *steps behind* **WIN**, *now making* **WIN** *first in line*

VOICE.

   Next!

WIN.

   Um. Hello hi hola.

   We–

VOICE.

   Which form?

WIN.

   – *(Wincing)*

   B?

VOICE.

   (Pause) Section?

WIN.

—

Eee-leven?

Eleven.

VOICE.

—

Status?

WIN.

Pending?

VOICE.

Nature?

WIN.

Normal.

VOICE.

Placement

WIN.

Unspecified!

> *A loud buzzer sounds*
>
> *The window disappears like a guillotine*
>
> **WIN** *in panic looks around for the exit*
>
> *Where is the exit??*
>
> *The buzzer stops*
>
> *The window opens and* **CIGARETTE MAN** *leans forward*
>
> *Is it same cigarette smoker as before, or is it a new one?*
>
> *He appears more cancerous than previously*
>
> *His teeth are rotting out*
>
> *After a long moment he speaks*
>
> *His voice comes from an electro-larynx*

CIGARETTE MAN.

Placement.

Unspecified?

WIN.

(Smiles) My Engaleash and me is sooo pour.

CIGARETTE MAN.

(To **PAN***)* You.

Have we met?

PAN.

I – we are looking to – for. Friend.

Small one girl. Her name of – is Noon.

She is go.

We. I think she can be. On your list?

CIGARETTE MAN.

—

PAN.

To go. For re-umm-reeeee –

(To **WIN***??)* – mmm –

WIN.

– Resettlement

PAN.

Yes.

CIGARETTE MAN.

No.

PAN.

No?

WIN.

(Whisper) Ok now you see, we can go.

To **CIGARETTE SMOKER**

WIN.

Thank-you-wel-come-come-again!

PAN.

You are sure?

CIGARETTE MAN.

Never can be sure.

–

Maybe I can pull some strings.

–

Care for a tickle?

WIN.

–

Hahaha.

CIGARETTE MAN.

Haha. Ha.

Or, how about candy?

I know you like candy?

Care to play?

> *A bolt latch unlocking from underneath the window*
>
> *The bottom section of the wall swings open*
>
> *Out steps the* **CIGARETTE MAN***. He is naked from the waist down*
>
> **WIN** *and* **PAN** *stiffen like prey might, and not like puppets*
>
> **CIGARETTE MAN** *lingers. Very subtly he presents himself to them*
>
> **CIGARETTE MAN** *holds out a hand and a piece of candy*
>
> *A moment.* **PAN** *takes the candy*
>
> **CIGARETTE MAN** *smiles and exits into the wall closing it behind him*
>
> *Cigarette smoke. The window shuts slowly*
>
> *Another opposite wall opens.* **WIN** *and* **PAN** *exit through it*
>
> *The city is smoke & mirrors*

WIN and PAN walk through them removing them disguises

WIN see shadow and face of THOM in smoke & mirror setee

No sign of NOON where

No sign of she

No not

–

–

She gone

Back at dump site

We sure it same?

But

But no garbages anywhere to see it

Where it went to?

PAN looking sicker and no panic but WIN a frenzy

Run aroundabout to looking

Where go it?!

WIN.

Where go it?!

(*To PAN*)

Where our home?

No tears

No tears never

PAN.

I no know.

Long minute waiting

WIN will cry?

No

No

Ye–

PAN.

No! I know.

PAN throw disguises to ground

PAN go in at audience corral

Walking in out seats beg "hello-hello"

PAN steal presents of garbages from audience

PAN go back to dump site and pile up

PAN make a pretty pile for WIN

WIN smile

WIN leave

> **WIN** *come in back with big theater cans filled of garbages*
>
> **WIN** *dump garbages all everywhere*
>
> *So pretty piles*
>
> *Too many garbages*
>
> **WIN** *and* **PAN** *swim in garbages*
>
> **WIN** *and* **PAN** *play in garbages*
>
> **WIN** *and* **PAN** *is back home*
>
> **DEVELOPER** *in hardhat enter follow behind two Laborers*
>
> *Measuring chalk line reel round dumpsite*
>
> **DEVELOPER** *chalkline over* **WIN** *and* **PAN**

WIN.

Hello. You want tea?

We no more tea here.

We finish all tea everywhere over.

Hellõ?

Hallo?

Hola.

Schwa.

Sveikischwa.

Nĭ hǎo.

Hujambo.

Guten tag.

Fǎverflaützè.

Bonjour.

Yo!

DEVELOPER.

(See nobody) Meh? Meh meh.

> **WIN** *and* **PAN** *hopping to get attention*
>
> *No luck*

DEVELOPER.

(See nobody) Meh meh meh meh. Mehmeh. Middle-class Meh mahhme Meh. Meh.

Structural adjustment. Meh. Meh MEH.

> *(A funny)*

Mehmehmehmehmeh! mehmehmoney-money mehmehmeh!

Me. Me. Meeehh. MEH! Meh mee mmeeh. Mehh me meh meh? Mmmmm?

–

Meh.

> *Laborers enter and are been directed to working*
>
> *Laborers is building infrastructure of building:*

A housing project; a peace-building

Much tools zip zapping and zap zipping and 2-by-4 wood fall crash

down and chalk line reel and mop bucket clean up and tape measuring and etc. etc. etc

Other ones to enter and join in social promotion and building

BABY BOO *breakdance*

W.H.O. *inoculating*

BACKPACKER *photographing to all it*

MILITIA *pulling at pet* **MIME** *on the leash.* **MIME** *miming*

GOSPEL CHOIR *ad-libs and so much window-washing hands while sing*

DEVELOPER *grab one audience to wear extra hardhat new* **DEVELOPERS**

Within the "meh-meh" chorus now, some strange foreign words invade:

"Resource curse"   "Innovation"

"Anti-oppression"

"Feminist-approach"   "Local buy-in"   "Bootstraps"

"Strategic planning"   "Poverty   "Profit-sharing"
                            reduction"

"Hope"   "Stakeholders"   "Investment strategies'

"Livelihood"   "Community-based"   "Target markets"
                                            "Corporate social responsibility"

"Enterprise"   "Individual agency"

"Free trade"   "Human capital"

"Training of trainers"   "Development goals"

"Empowerment"   "Beneficiaries"   "Income and outcomes"

              "Financial aid"   "Venture capital"

Soonish, only these words remain, until

Overhead

Thundercracker!

No rain

Thundercracker!

No rain

Farts!

Angel music ++

NOBLE LAUREATE *descend from sky*

She wearing most elaborate ultra color tradition dresses and multi-national brands

She be very pale-face like dead but revive and clean-shaven

Her long neck longer

And around it the giantest gold blings

One too longer a ring, with different shape hang down as medal award

PAN *with diamonds in very sad sick eyes*

All people in awe and collective inhale

PAN.

Are you

W.H.O.

She is

DEVELOPER.

You are?

NOBLE LAUREATE.

I am.

MILITIA.

–

Hey kid. Who that?

PAN.

She is. Fame-ly.

She is our fame-ly.

DEVELOPER.

Excuse me, do you have a work permit?

Or is this an unauthorized entry–

Thundercrack! Boom boom!

NOBLE LAUREATE.

Silence!

Farts!

NOBLE LAUREATE.

(Self-surprise) Wow. I'm. Here?

Wowuh!

Their chains could not hold me.

Ha! I'm no puppet.

I died? I

went Abroad. But now, returned. Reincarnate.

Familiar. Foreign.

The remnants of my past lives?

I was dead to the world but not now I'm back.

With a purpose. And, remittances?

What I've seen. I've gone the furtherest one can go. Beyond Here. After?

Beyond Past the edges of our known frontiers. I'm the final foreigner.

The Beginning the End the Alpha the Omega le Commencement et la Fin.

Every letter and language, I am.

Midnight, Mourning and Noon – no. I'm *after* Noon. I'm the future.

> **NOBLE LAUREATE** *take out pocket compact and prims*

PAN.

She is here.

> *(to* **WIN***)*

See we found her!

I knew we found her!

NOBLE LAUREATE.

No one found me I founded myself, I'm a founder. Self-made.

Listen to my commands – listen to my command of Engaleash, isn't it money?

Heed my density, behold my dexterous locution.

Supercalifragallisticexpialidocious, you're welcome. But *are* we?

Be on your best behavior – or they'll grab you in your sleep.

Hold the fork and knife when you eat.

Eat EngLEASH and speak it with consequence while smiling

at your hands. Be Godly.

Goodly. Be me.

In my many lives I discovered a thing or two – earned. Merit.

I have fourteen degrees, eleven certificates and eight lifetime achievement awards.

I'm known for being outgoing and vulnerable, but what I'm most proud:

I'm noble.

I've been lauded I'm a laureate, yes.

A noble laureate. Thrice.

For my unproven merit I won a Noble Peace Prize.

For my noble attempt at flight – I won the Prize in Physics.

AND I got a Noble Prize in Economics. Cuz I'm rich bitch!

Yes, and you're welcome. To worship me. Sing my praise,

celebrate my transcontinental assets.

I'm a stateless corporation you can't even touch because I'm untouchable.

I'm a brand, ready to give back because those tax-breaks are the bomb!

> *A bomb go off in far away*
>
> *Farts*
>
> *Foreigners collective inhale*
>
> *They so helium high on them drugs*

NOBLE LAUREATE.

I'm Here, Born Again!

A savior, sent to save the children.

–

Specifically to save:

> (*To* **PAN**)

You.

WIN.

Save Pan?

From what?

NOBLE LAUREATE.

From what, from who – Whom?

(*To* **PAN**) Look how sickly you've become.

They long to poison your innocence.

To extract your natural resources. But they don't know

where the gasses lays. Lays? Lies. Where the – lies?

PAN.

–

Lay.

NOBLE LAUREATE.

Exactly. You know. You're exceptional.

Haven't you had that natural feeling,

something bubbling up inside?

–

The gas: it's you. It's me.

The gas resides within us.

>   *Farts!*

>   *Collective inhale everybody*

NOBLE LAUREATE.

That's right, breath it in. Let my youth intoxicate you.

Children are the closest thing to god that's why we kneel to pray.

Be Ye all, uplifted! By the hot-air of my *(Sung)* fitted panties –

– Aaah awwh, will somebody get me something to *(Stand on)* –

>   *Someone bring* **NOBLE LAUREATE** *ladder or other ascendent thing*

NOBLE LAUREATE.

(Relief) Aaaahhhh. Much better.

–

Now no time to waste, we've got problems to solve.

First, we'll dismantle the welfare state. Then –

>   *Someone whispa to her something*

NOBLE LAUREATE.

O. We already did?

Great. Then we're well on our way.

We'll use the master's tools to remantle the master's house, then live in it.

A peace-building, courtesy of our corporate sponsors.

A big BIG house made out of gold bars, and merit.

A meritocracy where we write the rules and write the wrongs.

Do you see it? The new revolution?

Allow me to see on your behalf from my ascendant position.

I will stand up for you, while swinging precariously a little bit above you.

Give me your tired, your poor.

I shall be their monument, a model, a prayer.

Now. Pray!

>   *Foreigners all puja-pray in separate languages*

NOBLE LAUREATE.

(To **PAN***)* Come with me.

I only long to show you a New World.

Leave Here. Come, to the Hereafter.

In death there are no limits, only dreams.
We didn't create these borders someone else did.
It's time WE rewrite history. And I see that writing on the walls.
Soon, the oceans will disappear. *(Smiles)*
And our land will be realigned as it never was before, en masse.
Every crack and crevice that separates us will come together
in One. Mass. Movement. A landmass, a continent I will name after...you.
Our humblest fool: Pan.
Pan's-gia? Pangea.

> *Softly tambourines we hear*
>
> *And where that church organ sound come from?*

NOBLE LAUREATE.

Yes. A mass movement of endless mobility.
And there will be no rugged, outlying ice caps left because we will have
all melted into one. And there will be no overseas to go over
because the segregation of water will have vanished.
In our new smelting pot, every citizen will be an ethnically ambiguous actor.
And ethnically ambiguous actors will be the only actors we employ.
Because they will be happy to be in meaningful work. Finally!
Our minor majority will help build a world with no complaints.

> **GOSPEL CHOIR** *"Amen"-ing and "Preach preacha"-ing*

NOBLE LAUREATE.

And we, once repatriated on this immense, dry landscape,
will pledge allegiance to a more meaningful flag. One redesigned
to inspire confidence, hope and obedience.
Par dieu, I have a dream today!
There will be no more names people mispronounce.
I dream there will be no need for hand-shaking nor bowing of heads.
Greetings will be obsolete in the afterlife – nay abolished.
This is the oppressor's language. Therefore
unless spoken by me speeching will be forbidden, unnecessary,
as you will know everything you need to about anyone just by looking at them.
And from these great suspicions we will become a visionary society.
One spawned from my celebrated intellect, and these, my virgin loins.

> *(Farts! Farts!)*

And these same said loins will take you places you never dreamed.
Feverish, unfamiliar exploiting the distant edges of the Hereafter.
And there is where we will invest. And conquer.
And deliver unto us: Upward mobility.
No more this standing still?

(Sing) WE SHALL OVER–
(Spoken) – invest in mobile and that mobility shall drive us.
We will make progress unforgiving, unrelenting and fun.
And everywhere we go twill be a party.

Cuz our movement, twill make a Party.

One. Big. Party. And everyone is invited – nay forced to attend.

And there will be favors. And tickling. And dancing. And lights.

And streams of joy trickling down.

And most of all: there will be mobile phones with buttons.

And those mobile phones will broadcast the revolution.

And that mobility will lead us up up UPward.

And everyone will be made to buttress me from below.

A new world ruled by forced-upward-mobility and its power to transport, Par dieu!

– By jingo, I have a dream.

A prosperity theology! You get a car and you get a car and you get a car.

And free, unlimited gas for everyone.

(Farts! Farts!)

The Hereafter will be a place where everyone drives away a winner.

The Hereafter will be a place where everyone is entitled to Win.

(Farts! Farts!)

WIN.

I god! This, // is my purpose-driven life in this life and the next,   hey

and the next, and the next, and I will keep returning incarnate

to realize this, my sole aim.   excuse me?

To make it rain! Make it rain!

> **NOBLE LAUREATE** *with money make it rain down from heaven*
>
> *Foreigners grabbing like mad with fever*

NOBLE LAUREATE.

(To **PAN***)* Come my child.   **WIN.**

It's rainy season up in here!   hello?

You feel it? It's trickling down!

It's tricklin–

WIN.

HELLO, LADY!

NOBLE LAUREATE.

You dare interrupt me!!

–

I mean: yes?

WIN.

Keep it.

NOBLE LAUREATE.

Keep what?

WIN.

Keep "what," keep "who," keep all you words. You promises.

We no want.

NOBLE LAUREATE.

What do you mean? Everybody wants something.

WIN.

I mean I say, I no want. Whatever you is selling is.

DEVELOPER.

What is wrong with you boy, she is selling you a free car?!

W.H.O.

(Shaking pill bottles, holding inoculator) Maybe he prefers to ride the smile train.

WIN.

(To **NOBLE LAUREATE***)* You. Disappear?

Where you go you, Father?

Was never send to me one message.

No one letter, Father. Not one.

Why?

Now you here with you futcha pitcha.

–

Father.

Can you give me my Father?

Can you give me my Mother to me? Again?

Bring back my Sister. My atha Sister.

Re-alive, my Brother.

My friend so many, who all is all –

Gone?

NOBLE LAUREATE.

–

DEVELOPER.

(Whispa) –

If you don't want that free car can I have it?

WIN.

No.

No we no not want you car.

No want you train.

Your freedom words. You promises.

We is okay here, we. Happy.

> *(To* **PAN***)*

Yes?

> **PAN** *is silence*

NOBLE LAUREATE.

(To **PAN***)* Are you? Are you happy my old friend?

–

Come crossover with me?

Here, the Gods will never abandon you.

All you have to do is smile.

WIN.

Away all! NOW!

The show is finish. Clap clap clap Goodnight.

Off to you wherevers.

Forget us again. You have come and you will go.

> **WIN** *drag* **PAN** *to go inside tent tarp*
>
> *All else is unsure*
>
> *Someone, small clap clap*
>
> *Some movement*
>
> *One by one by two or more they exit*
>
> **NOBLE LAUREATE** *left hang-sitting in midair*

NOBLE LAUREATE.

    –

    –

Will someone help me. Down from here?

> *Light darken to night*
>
> *Shadow of Foreigner appear*
>
> **WIN** *wake see shadow and clench to sickle as weapon*

WIN.

Stay away! Go!
You no welcome here.

> *Shadow approach*
>
> *It is* **THOM**
>
> *He hold small suitcase one*

THOM.

Jack? Jack it's me.

WIN.

I see. I know.
You are like them.

THOM.

What?

WIN.

You. Go. Too.

THOM.

Yes.
I hear the fighting has increased.
Rumors of war, right across the border there.
You should leave this place.
You should leave with the others.

WIN.

I am not other. I am here.
I am of Here, not other.
I am stay You are go.
We do not want you.

THOM.

What? Of course we do.
You want me and I want you.

Remember?
You helped. Me to find myself,
to be who I am.
I gave you gifts. A name.
And language.
Your life before was...
It wasn't.
You've been reborn. Through how I taught you.
I helped.
And with that, you can now teach someone else.
You're welcome.
–
Jack–

WIN.

Jack, it not my name.
My name, Win.
I, Win.
I. Am. Win!

> **PAN** *appear from tent*
>
> **THOM** *move forward*
>
> **WIN** *raise sickle*

WIN.

Stop. I not going anywhere you!

THOM.

Jack, I *am* not.
I am not going anywhere *with* you.

WIN.

No Jack am I not. Not going.
Not I Win –

THOM.

I'm not here for you.

> **THOM** *handout to* **PAN**
>
> **PAN** *go to* **THOM**
>
> **THOM** *hand brushing* **PAN** *hair*

THOM.

Hello.

> **THOM** *kneel down give candy to* **PAN**
>
> **WIN** *drop sickle, snatch hard to* **PAN** *arm and pull him to away*

WIN.

You what you do?

PAN.

I leave. I will leave.

WIN.

With him? You cannot

PAN.

Yes.

WIN.

No. Please.

–

We are fame-ly.

PAN.

Are we? Were we?

WIN.

We are only fame-ly left.

–

We are brothers.

PAN.

My brothers are dead.

All. You know.

WIN.

But me. I am–

PAN.

You will be good.

You are.

WIN.

He is bad man.

PAN.

I know.

I know he is.

(Pointing)

Right over there.

Across the road. There are many bad men.

Many sad eyes. Red teeth.

Wolves like sheep. They smile while drinking blood.

Those men: they are worse. Much.

I do not want to meet these men when they come.

WIN.

Then we will togetha, fight to them. We. Us.

PAN.

No.

I want–

In my dream. I look and I see.

I dream of one big house. Not three.

One beautiful, big house. For all of us.

–

–

I won't forget you. I cannot.
One day, I may come back.

WIN.

You won't.
No one ever come back.

–

You Engaleash is so improve.

PAN.

You. Were a good teacher.

WIN.

No.

–

I want to unlearn you.

–

–

What did we speak before we spoke Engaleash?

> **PAN** *from pocket unfold Noon's pictcha-draw*
>
> **PAN** *give* **WIN** *pictcha-draw*
>
> **PAN** *and* **THOM** *go away, no fanfare*
>
> **WIN** *look at pictcha*
>
> **WIN** *is waiting for what?*
>
> *Empty is air and quiet like death*
>
> **WIN** *stands but does not pose*
>
> **WIN** *lay with* **NOON** *pictcha-draw*
>
> **WIN** *is look like garbages*
>
> *In the far distance, the sounds of urban warfare approaching*
>
> *nearer*
>
> *nearer*
>
> *Louder*
>
> **WIN** *with sickle stand up*

WIN.

I win.

–

I win.

–

I. Win.
I, Win!
I–

End of Play

Fitted Panties

(Standard)

Lyrics: Phillip Howze
Music: Wishnok and Phillip Howze

Fitted Panties

(Gospel)

Lyrics: Phillip Howze
Music: Wishnok and Phillip Howze

Samuel French

Fitted Panties - p.2

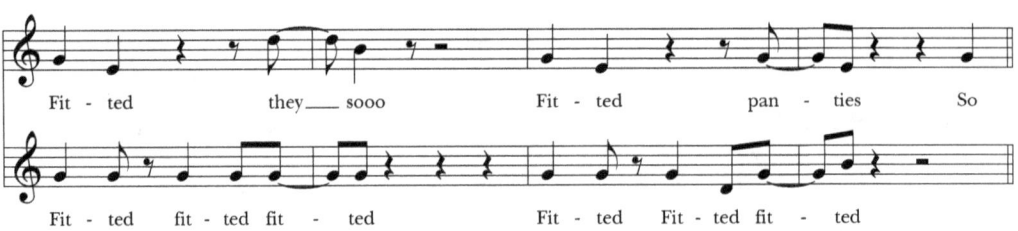

Fit - ted   they__ sooo   Fit - ted   pan - ties   So

Fit - ted   fit - ted fit - ted   Fit - ted   Fit - ted fit - ted

D

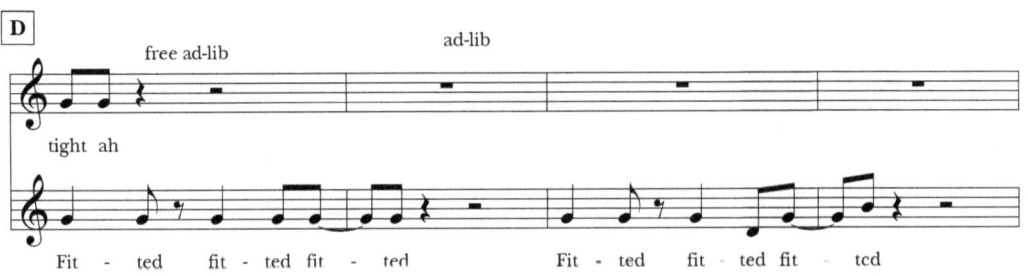

free ad-lib   ad-lib

tight ah

Fit - ted   fit - ted fit - ted   Fit - ted   fit - ted fit - ted

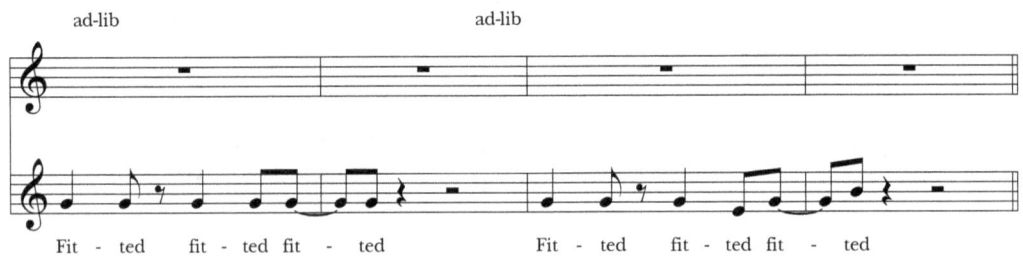

ad-lib   ad-lib

Fit - ted   fit - ted fit - ted   Fit - ted   fit - ted fit - ted

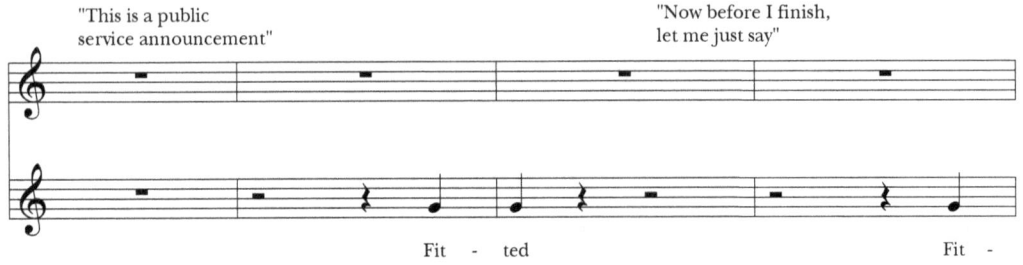

"This is a public   "Now before I finish,
service announcement"   let me just say"

Fit - ted   Fit -

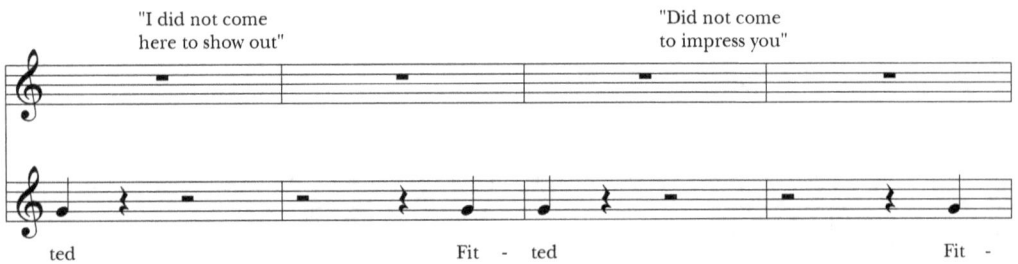

"I did not come   "Did not come
here to show out"   to impress you"

ted   Fit - ted   Fit -

Samuel French

Fitted Panties - p.3

"And I don't care what you think?"

"And I don't care what you think girl!"

ted

Fit – ted

Fit –

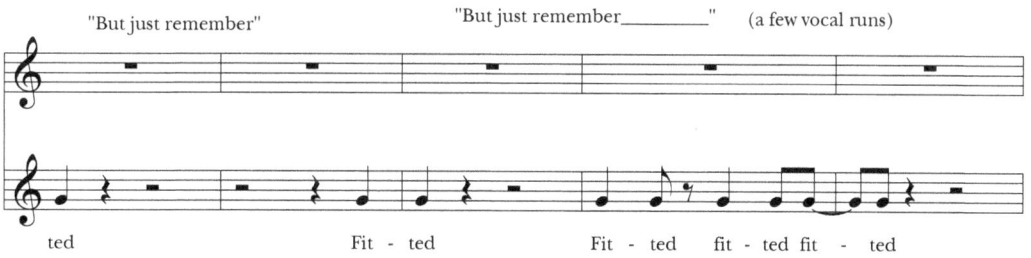

"But just remember"

"But just remember_____"   (a few vocal runs)

ted

Fit – ted

Fit – ted   fit – ted fit – ted

♩=60

Fit – ted   fit – ted fit – ted

aa – aa   aa – aa_____